I0445370

SWINGERS SEX STORIES
EXPLICIT DIRTY EROTICA SHORT STORIES

BREANA KHOR

CHAPTER 1

ACCEPTING SWING FUCKING

AYSIA WALKED into the art party frowning. She wore a Black Sabbath T-shirt and white stretch jeans that showed every curve below her hips and waist. Her black T-back sandals covered her black painted toenails. She carried a small cross-the-chest purse. The platinum blonde Agnostic Metal Head hated lectures about life and its purpose. She didn't believe in anything but good fucking. Unfortunately, she was single, having dumped her boyfriend recently. She held a chardonnay in her hand staring at what looked like a dick inside a vagina, turning her head sideways. "I don't get it. I just don't get it," she said, thinking she was alone by herself staring at the painting.

"It's a dick and cunt fucking," said an anonymous male voice coming up behind her. He wore blue jeans and a light-blue polo shirt, more fitting for a company picnic than an art show. He wore sandals on his feet because it was the middle of July.

"Yeah, I get that." She pointed her Chardonnay at the huge painting, almost big as half a door.

"Why so big? It's like those people who fuck in swing parties. I just could never admit to saying I like fucking at swing parties." She took another sip of her drink.

"I'd love to fuck at a swing party. If I was ever invited. As to bigger--" the young guy replied. "Bigger always better," said the voice with an Asian accent coming behind the two. "Women always want bigger." Cindy cast a knowing look at Aysia.

Aysia, turned back to look at thirty-year-old blue-hair Cindy.

She buried her smile in her drink again. "I--" Aysia stopped talking for a second. Then she droned, "I've had bigger and it's not all that." She took another sip looking her grape-blue eyes into the grey eyes of Cindy.

"Is a bigger cunt better for you?"

He jerked his chin back as if dodging a gnat. "Never thought about a bigger cunt," he involuntarily licked outward at Aysia.

Aysia sneered in disgust. "Tighter cunt."

Max approached the trio. He pulled up Cindy's China-doll white hand and kissed her knuckles. "My wife's cunt is not only big but tight."

They went around saying who they were. The young

man Matteo wore his brown hair in a buzz cut. He was single.The bored platinum blonde was Aysia. She recently dumped her boyfriend and needed something to occupy her free time.

They discussed the object in depth.

"The one thing we can say," bored Aysia finally concluded, "It is art. It's caused us to stand here, drink and discuss this piece of trash for thirty minutes."

Matteo laughed, "I could get used to your sick sense of humor Aysia." He pulled her close to him, but Aysia looked aslant at him and leaned backward. Aysia said, "No offense, but I'd fuck you, but my cunt might be too big for you."

"I doubt it," Matteo argued back.

Slowly, Aysia smiled.

"Why don't we all go back to our place," Cindy stole the opportunity to turn it into a swinger's bliss.

"Yes," Max said, nodding. "We can put dick to snatch and see how things fit together." "I'm game," said Aysia.

"I'm in," said Matteo.

"Now before we all get too excited," Cindy said, "This is a swinger's party. Everyone's coupled off." She waited in silence.

Aysia turned to Matteo. "I think we--" she pointed her Chardonnay to Matteo, who looked nervous. "We can--act like--a--couple to enjoy free--fucking."

Matteo suddenly smiled, as if realizing the gorgeous bored platinum blonde found him exciting after all. "You said it!"

Back at Cindy and Max's penthouse apartment, Aysia excused herself to the bathroom to pee. Cindy replied, "Too late. Max, my husband, already beat you to it."

"I really have to go," Aysia said, closing her legs and bending her knees together. Her palm reached down between her legs.

Cindy took charge. "Max! Cindy has to go!"

"What do you think I am a faucet? I can't just cut it off!" Max said from behind the dark oak bathroom door.

"I really need to tinkle! Max heard it was Aysia.

"In that case..." Max opened the door. His six-inch flaccid dick stood out nearly hard. "There you go." He held his dick straining. A pained expression on his face.

Brunette Aysia blushed. "I can't." "Sure you can," Cindy said.

"I don't know if she can," said Max. His dick was growing too hard to release his fluids, as he stared at the tight jeans of Aysia. Her bending over two times gave her a nice camel toe. He thought he even saw her clit form an impression against the forgiving material.

Cindy giggled uncontrollably and left to talk to Matteo.

Aysia moaned, "I must!" She forced down her jeans. Her tiny white panties had about ten blue, white and pink tiny flowers sprinkled on them. In the middle of her panty crotch was her pad. Aysia's pussy loudly gushed like a horse pissing and her yellow liquid entered the commode. Aysia cast her eyes in defiance up at fifty-year-old Max. "My period is over now!" "Does the job for me!" Max muttered. "You won't see me complaining." His dick was so hard precum leaked from the tiny slit of his bulbous cockhead. Max laughed.

Aysia laughed. "I don't know why tinkling is so embarrassing. We all do it." Aysia spread her legs as the piss continued to ring like music against the water below. She started stroking her clit and pulling up her clitoral hood. "I don't know about Cindy, but pissing makes me so fucking horny. I'm like a wench in need of a lollipop."

Max stepped forward.

Aysia took the hard pink, eight-inch love candy pole between her lips and started sucking. Her fingers jacked Max's cock up and back. She stopped. She looked down into the commode. "I think I'm almost done!"

However, Aysia went back to furiously sucking Max's cock. She bent his old strong dick up against his belly button. Aysia licked his cock from base to tip. "Mmmmmmmmm. I needed this lollipop after seeing that disgusting art piece." "That art piece turned me on, too," Max said, closing his eyes and gently rocking back and forth. He let her do all the work. His balls tightened on his groin.

. . .

"Let me relieve the pressure," Aysia said, noticing Max's heavy breathing. "This is the time for a young girl to show her stuff."

Aysia pulled his heated ball sacs lower, gently, little by little. Finally, after five minutes of hot sucking Max relaxed. "I don't think I'm going to come now. I can't believe it!"

"Simple physics. You can't come if your balls are loose." Aysia let his dick fall out of her mouth. "I finished tinkling."

"I'm sorry, but I can't piss until this hard-on disappears."

"I've just the vice for that pole." Aysia flushed the commode. She stood up, turned around, and leaned over the rich towels, bath and body products of the eccentric swinging couple. She turned over her shoulder. She pulled her long straight platinum blonde hair over her right shoulder by her breasts. "Have at it. Stuff that big cock inside this small tight cunt."

Max's eyes grew wide when she said that. "I thought you were serious. About big cunts." "I will be after you open me up, Max."

They got to rutting and fucking. At the same time, Aysia heard Cindy and Matteo fucking. Cindy screamed she couldn't take nine inches. Then said, "Fuck me more! Matteo."

The doorbell rang, and Max said, "Shit I'll have to get

that. The swing parties are about to begin. Don't move. Even if someone wants to fuck you."

"I won't move, but you better be the first cock inside my tight pussy. Or I'm never coming back."

"I won't let you down, Aysia."

Max came back and fucked Aysia until they both satisfied their lust. Then they fucked the other couples there: Clarissa and Hans, Tajh and Dejah, Nina and Reina, and of course Matteo and his wife.

CHAPTER 2

COFFEE, TEA, OR ME SEX

A SOFT MORNING light shined on the couples on the big super bed of Cindy and Max Harris. No music played. A wild Arizona bird chirped outside their penthouse window. Nina's left leg lay on top of Cindy's right leg. Nina's right leg lay on top of Max's left leg. Nina's right arm hooked under the elbow of her best friend Reina who started her swinging in the first place. Hans's dick rested on Nina's left cheek. Hans' throbbing dick. His seven-inch pussy splitter wanted more mouth action from Nina or one of the other ladies present. Max's soft cock lay under the closed fist of Reina's right hand. Reina dreamed of stroking Max's fifty-year-old cock again and again until it erupted in a white hot shower over Alysia's ass, now turned down on the bed beside Max. Alysia's right side brushed against Matteo, also on his stomach. Matteo's right upper arm covered Dejah's left breast. His hand palmed Dejah's right breast. Tejh's mouth lay between Alysia's dripping pussy crotch.

. . .

The Professional Swing Group, as they called themselves, lay peaceful. Cindy Wanton's eyes fluttered. She mumbled in her sleep something she rarely does. "The Sun rises--you'll see," she said quietly. Her voice trailed off. Her optimism was always infectious to white-haired Max, who made his millions in plastics, containers, and kitchenware. Max turned slightly before sleeping again.

Nina heard the chipper Asian voice of Cindy, the grand dame of their swing group. She moaned. She became aware of her own sexy body. Cindy Wanton Harris' hand eased down to her pussy lips. Her clit throbbed with need. A touch. A lick. A suck. Cindy thought she was horny.

Nina was the horny one.

Nina wanted to wake up. Grogginess perplexed her brain. What had she done last night? Who had she fucked? How many guys? How many girls? Where was Renia? The last thing she remembered Reina saying was that she met this nice interracial couple, Asian Cindy Wanton and Max. Like a rag doll trying to figure out where the string ties were, Nina turned inward. Her pussy drooled like a faucet. Her right leg lay on top of Max's left leg. Her right arm hooked under the elbow of her best friend Reina. Her left leg lay on top of Cindy Wanton Harris' right leg. *I have to wake up,* Nina chided herself.

Renia crawled over everyone and lay on top of Nina. She kissed Nina.

Nina turned her head away, she squinted her eyes. "It's too early and your breath smells like sperm."

Nina giggled. "Your breath smells like sperm and pussy sleepyhead." Nina reached slowly down and started easing her graceful hand-model hand to Nina's crotch. "What a messy wet pussy slit you have, Nina." She pulled apart the sticky cunt hairs, full of dried sperm and girl oils. "I want to fuck this pussy for the third time."

Nina shook her head no. "I'm too sleepy. I can't...I can't wake up...I need coffee--"

Reina ignored her. She now had her best friend Nina pinned to the mattress. Breasts to breasts, groin to groin, both bellies pressing against one another in their monthly needs, which synced up a year ago. "I know you want it. You're ovulating. Like I am." Reina panted as her forefinger pried at last past the dried cum barrier and reached the slippery girl's wetness within. Reina smiled, looking down at Nina's gorgeous body. Reina pumped her slender finger inside Nina, awakening her needs again. Awakening Nina.

Nina's head started clearing, but something replaced the fogginess. Pussy hunger.

Reina lowered her face and gently kissed Nina's left nipple. Not in a voracious hunger, but a gentle nudge, like a baby, might nudge a new mom's nipples. Nina raised up her chest afraid she would wake the others. "Nina. Nina . . . Stop . . ."

she whispered. "We might wake the others." Reina stopped kissing Nina's nipple for a second. "They're too tired to be awake. Only two nymphos like us can get up this early."

Nina smiled and closed her eyes again. She didn't want to be rude, but her body felt nice. Warmth spread throughout her body. Her pussy expanded again, growing inside, in both directions. Nina now happily accepted Reina's probing fingers. Fingers incessant, begging and taking all at once. This was going to be one explosive orgasm, Nina thought. Holding the passion pent up in her head, she was afraid she might yell out FUCK ME RENIA. FUCK ME MAX! FUCK ME MATTEO! FUCK ME HANS! "Coffee--" was all Nina could mutter as the first wave of her orgasm neared.

If she never mentioned making that porn film to Reina, they might not be here. Nina smiled and then silently gasped. Her back arched, sucking Reina's fingers deeper into her girly spaces. Nina wasn't the real nymphomaniac. Reina had the problem. Maybe it was all an act to get her into bed. Into her panties, Nina now thought. She loved the feel of Reina's weight against her body.

Too bad I'm not a lesbian. Reina would love that, Nina thought. She just liked to experiment from time to time. And fucking a girl never got her pregnant. Nina wanted to roll over and let Reina take her from behind like she always does. Using their big black dildo at home.

. . .

Nina groaned, "I need more."

Reina reached under Cindy and Max's mattress. She retrieved the massive twelve-inch-black- fuck dildo. Speaking really quiet, Reina cooed, "Open your eyes, my love. I found something like at home."

Nina opened her eyes playfully. Her eyes shot open. She awoke. "Fuck no!" she said in a hushed tone. "Where did you find that monster?"

"Now, Nina, you don't really care," Reina cooed, as she eased the tip into the open mouth of Nina.

Nina licked the monster's fake cock. Her pussy clamped down and drew back inside anticipating it. "Use it quick before someone wakes up!"

Reina glided the tool of pussy destruction down Nina's breasts. She moved on to Nina's belly button and jesting tried to stick it inside her tummy. "You're too tight. It won't fit! Damn!"

Reina said seriously, looking deep into Nina's frustrated eyes. Nina rolled her head from side to side carefully not to disturb the others. "Come on, Reina . . . Please!"

Reina moved the monster over Nina's clit bump of Nina and wiggled it. "Won't fit there either." She purred.

· · ·

"Mmmuuuuuummmm." Nina replied.

Reina gasped. "Oh, I think I found the right hole, Nina," Reina said after stopping briefly before Nina's pee hole and moving further downward. "This is the right open space. I'm positive."

Reina twisted the black monster cock back and forth inside the opening of Nina's swollen ruby fuck lips. Nina raised her legs slowly. Her pussy burped girl oils out and then Reina shoved that monster cock halfway home!

Nina's eyes shot open wider. Her eyebrows narrowed. The waterline of her eyes trembled as the huge instrument made further and further progress up her wet snatch."Ahhhhhhhh!" Nina let go in a near-silent scream.

Reina enjoyed the invasion as much as if the fake cock were her own. She pushed. She rammed. In and out.

Finally unable to stay quiet. Nina yelled. "I don't need coffee. I'm awake. I'm alive! I'm coming!" Nina screamed.

Max and Cindy woke up and ignoring them, Cindy said, "It's about time someone found my fake old man under the bed."

Max replied. "I agree. I was afraid he was going to scare one of the girls during the night." "These girls are bigger now, Max. They don't scare that easily anymore."

. . .

Nina screamed a second time as Reina covered her mouth with a kiss. Reina said, "I told you swinging was a good habit to have."

CHAPTER 3

CONDOM FUCK GAMES

MAX RAMMED HIS SECOND, then the third finger inside my cunt as I watched the Condom Fuck Games in the upper tier of the Budapest, Hungary stadium. Earlier, he covered my lap with our coats. I spread my legs wider. I wore a dark red cardigan sweater and no bra. With each move, my tiny tits were made visible by the clinging material. On my hips and bottom, I wore a simple white skirt and no panties. If I stood in front of a light, the hanging sex garden of my pussy flaps and clit became visible. "Fuck my Asian twat, Max! Stick your fist up my slippery pussy hole!"

Max's parents came from Hungary to the USA back in the twenties. While visiting one of them, the Condom Fuck Games came on satellite television. My eyes glazed over. My pussy melted. These were like the Olympics of fucking. Couples participated. Men and women did some activity, Judo, gymnastics or trampoline, horseback riding, and at the end, they had to fuck. Speed and a final mating always happened. A couple from Ukraine came onto the floor.

She was a beautiful Amazon German Blonde named Clarissa. Sexy and naked Clarissa rose on her toes repeatedly in preparation.

She stood five-foot-eight and 137 pounds and round B-cup tits bounced on her chest. Her partner was the big former weightlifting champion, Hans. Hans lay on the mat some fifty feet away. His cock jutted from his groin hard in 30 seconds. Clarissa lined up on the far end and waited for the whistle. It blew. The crowd roared. Clarissa pumped her arms. Camera angles focused briefly on her full red lips, her two thick blonde ponytails flying behind her back. Her B cup mams flopped back and forth on her chest. Her tall muscular legs charged forward. She looked like a Goddess. She was beautiful. Right away, I wanted to swing-fuck with Clarissa and Hans. But we had to be introduced first. In almost twenty seconds, Clarissa finished dashing across the red mat, reached the blue, and threw herself into two back handsprings across the blue mat.

She ran two gigantic steps across the green mat, front somersaulted, and landed her knees and legs spread astride Han's stiff cock. Amazingly, her puss slot, obviously wet, sucked Hans' cock down in three seconds. "A NEW CONDOM FUCK GAMES RECORD!" the announcer said.

By this time, I thrashed around in the black stadium seat. Max's fist pumped my sopping cunt. He leaned closer to cover our movements in a hug-kiss. His Royall Lyme aftershave cologne wafted with my own cunt smell. Juices ran down my quivering thighs. My shaved pussy humped against his fingers, thumb, and wrists. I mumbled, "Sun will rise--you'll see" right before my climax shook my body into bliss. Hans removed his thumb from my puss slot. His thumb slipped over my clitoris from every angle possible. I opened my glazed eyes as Hans planted the most passionate kiss on my lips in four years of marriage. For a second time, I came as the crowd yelled as Clarissa and Hans stood up and bowed. Hans' long cock on the big screen was slick in Clarissa's fuck sauces. I was so glad Max introduced me into swinging at that moment. Swinging feels a deep need. And I needed to fuck Hans as soon as possible.

"Personally, I do not know anyone there at your swing party," Hans said in his deep Ukrainian voice. He glanced at his friend, Clarissa.

"I not fucked in America yet, why not?" Clarissa urged.

In no time, we were on a plane back home to Arizona, to our place.

"This is a big place, Cindy and Max." Hans rolling deep voice filled our penthouse apartment. "Beautiful. Beautiful." Clarissa moved quickly through our private space. She called out from the bedroom, "Hans! Their bed is big enough for the Condom Games!"

Hans, Max, and I all laughed and followed Clarissa's German accent voice into the bedroom.

Clarissa started undressing right away. She dropped her sheath tiger-striped dress to the red carpet.

· · ·

"Red carpet for the bedroom. Emerald carpet for the living room." Hans said impressed. "We don't want to let the world know we're swinging," I said.

Max nodded. He took off his black muscle T-shirt and lowered his black jogging pants. "Red living room carpet would shout swingers."

I dropped my white skirt on top of my red cardigan sweater. I rubbed my own tiny tits in anticipation of Hans's quick fucking. Clarissa bit her lower lip. Max hefted his eight-inch cock, the largest in the room, besides my fake nine-inch black dildo under the mattress.

Almost like someone blew the whistle. I crawled onto the bed.

Quickly, Hans circled behind me. "What a fucking fine Scorpio tattoo on your lower back." He touched it for good luck, before dragging his finger up my thin hot pussy line. Hans licked his finger. Like lightening, Hans rooted his dick up my wet, wet, China Doll snatch. "Sun always rises, but sometimes shaded pink is better for it," I said.

Hans laughed. "See me in the morning China Doll." He pumped inside me again. Deeper he went as I expanded.

Clarissa lay on her back across the bed. Max positioned himself between her long pale legs. He lusted after her. He teased her by showing Clarissa every angle of his cock.

Clarissa sucked in her breath. "Give him to me!"

"The deep driller can't wait to fuck you--but first," Max said, jacking off and rubbing his delicious penis all around. His free hand pushed his white hair bangs from his forehead. His pink pool-ball nuts tightened. I watched him on my hands and knees. I bent low to ease the fierce frustration on Clarissa's face. "Max always jacks off to a woman before the first fuck. It helps lock her into his imagination."

"I'm not used to such delays. Uugggggghhh." Clarissa's hand brushed past her flat belly button and she pressed her middle finger on her clit twice. Madly she pushes the clit hood to its limits by rolling the slicken material in brief tiny circles.

I lowered my mouth on Clarissa's B-cup titties. Her nipples were swollen and hard. I sucked in hard. My tongue and cheeks brought her nipples to the roof of my mouth. I moaned around Clarissa's tits one after the other.

Hans' big hands held my plump ass cheeks apart. He was looking at my asshole. A mind-shattering feeling arose in my gut. He wanted to fuck my ass. Max and I'd never ass fucked. I felt a little humiliated. Hans spreading my plump ass cheeks. My covering. My covering for my cunt and virgin asshole. What if he just pulled out and took my ass? I started convulsing around his seven-inch pecker, the immense pleasure of my imagination driving me wild.

"You really like it dog style!" Hans growled and grinded deeper inside my pussy. He fucked me harder. He slammed into my plump ass. My ass jiggled back and forth when he let go to grope my tiny tits. He fucked me. He rocked me back and forth. I simply let my mouth stay open, my tongue hanging out and licking Clarissa's pink blushing tits up and back.

Clarissa whispered-moan, "Fuck me, Max, My pussy is lonely!"

Max's dick meat flickered glossy in the bedroom light from his precum near her pink pussy. I never saw such a pretty pussy. Her cunt looked like sushi, her cunt flaps even across. Her fuck hole is open like a begging mouth needing cock.

Max slid inside Clarissa's honey hole all at once. He placed his thumb on Clarissa's clit and in seconds, she was squeezing the bedsheets, biting the pillow as she screamed out her lustful come.

Then she started fucking like a crazy teenager. I lost track of all else because Hans found my clit. He drew my attention to every inch of my own sloppy cunt sounds. The smell of pussy sushi filled the bedroom as I lay on my left cheek and spent my come girly lubricants all over Hans Gamecock.

We rested for an hour. We repeated our stimulating madness in several positions and called it a night. That's how Max and I met the athletic Clarissa and Hans. I'll never forget it.

CHAPTER 4

THE CUNTY FAIR

I WAS beside myself with glee. It was the time of year when the autumn leaves turned from green to yellow and orange, where all the fun Friday night football games were being played, and yes, it was also time for the annual Cunty Fair. I had been the organizer for the Cunty Fair ever since it started 10 years ago. It wasn't your typical county fair that's for sure. It was a group of us swingers and wife and hubby swappers in town who wanted our own version of "playtime." We sponsored an event that made even the weakest dicks hard and the driest cunts wet. On top of that, most of the proceeds went to the children's cancer hospital here in town.

It was two days until the big Cunty Fair opened its gates and we still had quite a bit of preparation to do. I had booked our live entertainment as well. I tried to think of something to please all tastes. Also, thanks to the huge dona- tion by the Kiwanis club naughty clowns, we could afford none other than Ms. Bernadette Peters as our huge Saturday night performer. It also was beginning to look like the Kiwanis club clowns would be able to make a "secret" appearance as well this year at our fair. It was being held outdoors of course on a spacious 10-acre plot of land that was owned by the local nudists in our community.

You are more than likely getting a boner right now wondering what the fuck a Cunty Fair is. Feel free to browse our brochures and pamphlets of course, but in a nutshell, our Cunty Fair was an amazing and erotic rendition of the typical county fair held across this great nation we live in. At a typical fair, you play horseshoe toss. At our fair, we play toss the cock rings. At a regular old fair, you may bob for apples. At our fair, you bob for dildos. Maybe you are used to going to the freak show at your fair. At ours, you go the perv show and have your dick sucked off in the dark through a glory hole in the wall and our trick mirrors make your cock look 5 feet long.

I was in charge of the pin the cunt with a donkey dick venue, an amusing little adventure similar to the glory hole principle for men. Instead of them sticking their cocks through a hole in the wall, we had a velvet curtain draped over three women and charged $50 per man to come and stick their rubber-wrapped cock into one of the three lovely cunts exposed by holes in the curtain. We had bare cunts, hairy cunts, landing strips, and more. We had several volunteers waiting in the back more than willing to take their place underneath the curtain. I spied Dan and his wife walking into our tent, an old companion of mine, and watched with relish as he pulled out his long curved cock while his wife watched. I had held that cunt crammer before and knew it all too well for the pleasure it could provide. Dan picked the hole on the end, a deliciously hairy snatch with long protruding cunt lips. When he slid his lubricated cock into the end cunt a loud moan came from underneath the curtain. I couldn't help but think to myself...let the games begin!

The opening day of the Cunty Fair was one to behold indeed. The naughty couples came from far and wide to share a bit of lust and love with their neighbors. We had the dildo bobbing set up and it truly was pretty neat to see hot ladies trying to pick up dildos out of the water with their cunt lips. You'd be absolutely amazed about what some of these bitches could do with their impossible to believe but still real lengthy snatch lips. There was knotty Nina who could tie her lips in a knot and Spitting Suzie who could shoot a jellybean out of her cunt nearly ten feet. We have had such talent in the pussy department and the men were always so willing to spend their hard-earned money on a few girls. After all, it WAS for charity.

My favorite was Gushing Gilda, aptly named for her ability to squirt her cunt juice up in the air like a fountain. It didn't take Gilda much; a few rubs of her clit and a finger or two rubbed against her G-spot and man the lifeboats, here comes a flood! Then of course who could forget smokin' Rita? She had been a Cunty fair favorite since we started. There was a reason for that. Before the weekend would close Rita would be trying to break her record for smoking the most Camel filter cigs with her cunt. Last year Rita's hairy bush smoked a whopping pack and a half. Would Rita's greedy cunt beat its own record this year? She often liked to use a cigarette holder on her cigarettes but that only made her cunt look like Rita Hayworth with lip surgery so she saved that for her private showings.

One of the very favorite performances every year was by the cock clowns. There was Teeny, a midget with a cock that hung halfway to his midget kneecap.

· · ·

Skinny Wood's claim to fame was being the favorite in the cock ring toss event because he had once managed to get 14 rings on his upturned peter.

Big Hoss was aptly named for his prodigious member, which looked more suited to a quarter horse than a man. These clowns were loved by all at the Cunty fair and whenever they showed up in a tent there was always some fucking fun! When he pulled on that fucker it looked like a man milking a flotation device, and when he shot, you'd swear he had a gallon of clown goo hidden in his underwear. He'd spray down the tent and have the women running for cover as his huge load splattered the crowd.

The 10th annual Cunty Fair went off without a hitch and we all had a blast of fun and some big shots of cum. After the long weekend my cunt screamed for a week, she was so sore from being poked, fingered, sucked, and fucked!

CHAPTER 5

PROFESSIONAL SWINGER SEX

CINDY WANTON HARRIS' hand eased down to her pussy lips. "Max, Dear, see our athletic Clarissa." Cindy pointed a small finger at the Amazon blonde flipping her body into a handstand against their wall. Clarissa wore a white blouse and mini jean skirt, and no shoes. Her upside-down pink pussy lips glistened in the living room light of the Harris' penthouse home.

"Who wants first mouth fuckings?"

Clarissa's two thick German blonde ponytails touch the emerald green carpet floor. Her B-cup joy balloons pressed tight against the cotton material. Two pointed nipples poked outward against the garment.

"Clarissa, you've outdone yourself now." White-haired Max said. Then he chuckled. "If Cindy doesn't give me that blowjob swing party starter," he paused and turned to his wife of five years. Cindy's Asian eyes did a mirthful squint as she dropped to her knees. She was totally naked except for the Scorpio tattoo on her lower back, over her dimpled small plump ass. "I'd rush to plug your sexy mouth—OOOOhhhhhhhhhh. Awwwwweeeeeeeeeeeee! Damn Cindy that does the job. Now you are distracting me."

Hans's big voice boomed out. "I got this Max. You just—hmmm, Cindy you can vacuum some cock for an Asian chick—I'll give Clarissa a hot dong lunch to suck on."Hans and Clarissa used to like one another, but that's another story. However, as singles, they needed a sex partner to attend swinger parties.

"Bring your emo ass over here," Clarissa said, straining to hold her inverted position. "Not my cunt you! My other cunt. My mouth you big dolt. Bring your main muscle down." Clarissa swallowed looking at the bronze color, Hans. Hans had big thick blonde hair. He tried to brush it back, but it fell over his forehead forming bangs.The two belonged together.

"MMmmmuumm" Clarissa swallowed and licked.

Hans kneeling fed his sausage into her broiler fuck mouth. "Sluuuurrrrrppp. Suuuuuccccccccckkkk Suucccckkkkk." Hans pulled out to give Clarissa some air to breathe.

"Sputtt! What do you do that for? I was just getting... started." She strained and pushed off the wall.

Bronze Hans caught her long thighs. His strong arms encircled her waist. He grunted as he stood up. "You gained some weight since our last Trojan Fuck Game Championship."

. . .

"I have not!" Clarissa snorted as her hands now off the emerald carpet, grabbed Hans' muscular weightlifter thighs. She freed one hand and grabbed Hans's seven-inch pussy fucker and shoved her mouth onto his hard meat. Her blonde ponytails swung in tandem back and forth. Her mouth slipped easily over his thick pecker sausage.

Max's knees almost buckled when he saw Hans and Clarissa's athleticism. He tapped Cindy on the cheek lightly.

Cindy pulled almost all the way from his cock. Her thin yellow lips held Max's cockhead only. Her tongue performed lazy circles around his bulbous fuck head. Cindy turned further sideways and forced Max's cock into her right cheek. Her tongue kept thrashing the length of his cock.

Cindy's free hand stroked her hot thin line of her pussy. She needed to cum. Watching others fuck always excited her clit and pussy flaps and cunt hole. Cindy stopped aghast for a second. She turned back and started sucking faster, harder. Her bob-cut blue hair flounced forward and back as her throat muscles worked overtime, stroking Max's fifty-year-old pink cock. Cindy's gray eyes looked upward at Max who could not maintain his focus on Clarissa and Hans.

Cindy's mouth joy rocked every nerve in the old business tycoon's healthy body. His huge balls tightened up under his groin. His breathing became rapid. His eyes rolled back in his white-haired head providing Cindy the assurance sought. She pulled off Max's cock and placed her hand around his fireplug dick. Fast as a jackhammer, Cindy's small yellow hand moved over and back on Max's thick fuck wong.

"Does the job—for me!" Max muttered as his sperm boiled hotter and hotter in his man sacs.

Cindy held her mouth open. Wide. . . Wider. Max peered down his finely chiseled nose and sent volcanic white sperm down her throat, over her front teeth, on her tongue, inside her left cheek, until at last, Max's penis shrank, shrank down like a deflated tube balloon.

Max dropped to his knees. He hugged Cindy his wife, "What did I ever do without you?" He exclaimed and they kissed, as Clarissa and Hans howled out their mutual orgasms as Hans hurried to the couch to let Clarissa down softly.

Cindy pulled one white towel from a stack of towels on the coffee table nearby covered in swinger magazines from different countries. She flipped the towel open. She laid it down on the carpet. She pushed Max onto his back and mounted him. Her slender yellow thighs straddled his hairy old legs. Cindy loved to dry hump.

Max smiled. "I'll be up in a hurry if you keep being so horny."

"Sun will rise, yes. I'm a dry humping Asian princess—remember." Cindy's five-feet-three body contorted in a sensually up and down fashion. Her breasts rubbed against the hairy chest of Max, then her belly, then her clit, and finally, she even managed to get his cockhead to nudge inside sloppy pesthole.

. . .

They met at an outdoor concert listening to loud classical music in the park. Max stood behind her holding his beer. Cindy noticed him trying to stare down at her cowslip pink blouse. She pushed back her tight ass in her black stretch pants, humping Max until he came during the crescendo of Handel's Fireworks.

Max wrapped his jacket around his waist and they went into Starbucks. Like teenagers, the odd couple hit it off right away. Later they went back to Max's large penthouse home and fucked like it was possibly the end of the world. Max and Cindy had been an item ever since.

Inseparable. However, after four years, their marriage threatened to evaporate completely. So

Max suggested swinging. Something he did a lot in his 30s with his previous wife. Cindy warmed up to the idea. She loved fucking near-strangers. Usually, they were people they knew, met, or developed a quick sexual attraction to. Currently, their swing partners were Hans and Clarissa, The Agnostic metal head Aysia. She wore band shirts like All That Remains and Black Sabbath. She talked down about others' music interests.

Tajh, from Croatia, was always backup to whatever Cindy wanted to do. He understood about keeping their swing set closed for now. Cindy wanted to get to know them all--better. And what better way to find out about someone than to fuck them! Tajh had black hair, eyebrows, and the bluest cobalt blue eyes. He loved to partner up with raven-haired Dejah from Romania. She had a small dog and always wore pink outfits. She hand-painted her nails animal prints, flower designs, and even famous footwear colors. She went to Princeton and has an MBA in business, and never went anywhere unless her hair was perfect.

Matteo, a scientist, used swinging to distract him from the dry sterile clean rooms he worked in. He loved to prove things true. Swinging made sense to Matteo. "People are not monogamous. I don't know why they try to be." He had brown hair and wore it in a buzz cut. Matteo loved to fuck Nina, the movie actor. She fucked the best he thought. Once she performed on film—as a porn star. She loves loud music, and rave parties. Just twenty years old, Nina, had changed her hair color more than fifty times.

Reina had blonde hair. Wore gym shoes a lot and had a fantasy about fucking older men. When Nina suggested she could fuck a rich man 30 years her senior, Reina jumped at the opportunity to join their swing group.

Everyone in their group fucked now. Reina and Matteo and Nina fucked in the Master bedroom, but that is another story. And Cindy loved to watch others fuck.

ABOUT THE AUTHOR

Breana Kohr is an emerging erotica author of many erotica kinks and sub-genres. Be sure to check out other books and leave a review if this story got you hot!

Visit my blog at Breana Kohr's Blog

Join my newsletter for the exclusive Breana Kohr's Newsletter

Sign up for Free Stories from Xplicit Press Authors

Xplicit Press Author Updates

Like Xplicit Press on Facebook

Follow Xplicit Press on Twitter

Readers: I want to expand a few of the stories to see where the characters can be explored further. If there are any of the stories that you would like to read more about again, I'd love to hear from you!

Keep In Touch
Breana Kohr
info@breanakohr.com